Colton's A

A Western

M.Allen

Chapter 1

Colton squared his shoulders. Sitting high on the back of his chestnut steed, he rocked along with each step they took. Dust kicked up around them, sticking to the sweat running down his face and saturating his shirt. His horse chuffed, blowing out a hard breath between his lips. Colton reached down, patting his hand over the horse's satiny main. "Easy, boy. I don't like it here any more than you do."

The stallion sidestepped, jostling Colton in the saddle. On any given day, his horse, Scorpion, was a mean son of a bitch. But put him in the center of a town bustling with activity, and he was downright dangerous. Scorpion's ears pressed back against his head as he yanked at the bit in his mouth. Colton pulled in the reins and squeezed his legs, urging his ride forward. The trek from his ranch in the Texas Territory to the Buckley settlement, clear on the other side of Texas, was some seventy miles away. After a long ride, all he wanted was a hot meal and perhaps a bath. Yet he rode on, searching for the youngest of his seven brothers, Jason.

Three weeks ago, he'd sent his brother to make arrangements with the biggest ranch in the area to use their land as a pass-through for their cattle. When Jason, or Jace as they liked to call him, didn't return, Colton did the only thing he could think of. He convinced his other brothers into staying put for two more weeks while he went hunting for Jace. If he didn't make it back before then... God help this territory. No one in their right mind wanted any of the Sutton men around.

The wind swirled down the street, covering the storefronts in dust. Colton pulled his hat low over his eyes, blocking the sand from hitting his face. When he reached the town center, he dismounted and tied Scorpion to a post outside the local watering hole next to a few other horses. When he took a step back, his stallion slammed his body into the animal next to him. The other horses stomped their hooves in a frenzy, neighing at Scorpion. They began yanking at their reins, all trying to pull away from the large beast.

Three men sauntered out of the swinging doors of the saloon and stood on the wooden planks leading into the establishment. With black hats pulled low, long leather dusters and about three days' worth of facial hair, they all looked identical lined up side-by-side. The man in the center took a small step forward. He rested his hands on his gunbelt and tapped his fingers on the pistol at his side. "That there's a fine looking stallion you got."

Colton nodded, narrowing his eyes at the gunslinger. A sizable bruise marred the side of the man's face. "That he is." When he looked toward the others, they also had cuts and bruises on each of their faces. *Jace...* His youngest brother had a way of ending up in a tussle.

"Careful you don't leave him there. Folks 'round here got a hankering for stealing horses." The man crossed his arms over his chest. The beat-up leather of his coat creased at his elbows. Even from this angle, Colton could see he had a good four inches on the man. The gunslinger held his shoulders back, his head high, as a smug smile split across his face. He smirked at Colton while running his hand over the scruff coating his face.

Colton rested his hand on his own gunbelt. "Is that a threat... friend?"

"If it was, you'd know it." The man chuckled, and like the lap dogs they were, the others with him followed suit.

"Then, by all means, have at him." Colton shrugged knowing his stallion had put many a folk in bandages. If these slingers had a lick of sense, they'd stay away.

The man gave a humorless scoff and tipped his hat. "I'll keep that in mind."

"Perhaps you boys can point me in the right direction?" Colton motioned his hand up and down dusty road.

"We ain't in the habit of givin' tours to strangers."

"I don't believe I'm a stranger to these parts. Now, if my brother ain't in that there saloon, then there's only one other place to find him." Colton pulled a hand-rolled cigarette from his pocket and lit the end. He took a deep drag, letting the smoke sit heavy in his chest before blowing it out toward the men he faced.

"There ain't no brothers 'round here." The slinger pointed his finger toward Colton's chest.

"Well, I don't know about that. You three look like you came from the same sack of shit." Before the men could reply, Colton turned while he chuckled and ambled down the street. "I best be headed to the jail."

"I'll be seeing you later… *friend*," the man bellowed at his back.

Colton turned and flicked his cigarette at their feet then tipped his hat. "I believe you will."

Wooden planks held each of the buildings off the dirt road, and at the end of the path, like a beacon, stood the church. The setting sun cast the shadow of the cross over him. He snickered to himself. If only his brothers could see him now... covered by the cross. A few more buildings down, he found the local jail just a small ways from the saloon. He pulled his dust covered hat off his head and smacked it over his chaps, knocking the dirt loose from it. The pouch full of coins hung heavy on the inside of his duster. He took the step up to the jail.

When he opened the door, he entered a square room with two cells sitting at the back of it and a broken-down desk in front. The portly sheriff rose to his feet, hiking up his belt. "What can I do you for?"

Colton looked to the cell to his left where his brother leaned against the bars, his dirty hands draped through the bars. He pointed his finger at Jace's chest. "You done cost me a weeks' worth of work to find your hide."

The youngest by barely a year, Jace held all the charm of a schoolboy with none of the manners. He stood covered from hat to boot in dirt and grime. Colton could still make out the Sutton features, which got him more female attention than a stallion surrounded by a pack of mares in heat. His dark brown hair hung over his brows, lines fanning out around his sapphire eyes.

4

When he caught sight of Colton, an ear-splitting grin came across his face. "'Bout time you got here, big brother."

Colton shook his head and faced the sheriff. "I'm here to ante up for him." He notched his head toward Jace.

The sheriff adjusted his belt and crossed his arms, resting them on his stomach. "I'm sorry, but he's being held for disturbing the peace, drunkenness, and starting a brawl."

"They had it comin'," Jace argued.

"Sheriff, he's an ornery pain in the ass. But we both know he ain't gonna swing for it." Colton tossed a sack of money on the desk. "How's about you take that there pouch, release my brother, then send us on our way?"

"You tryin' to bribe an official of the law?" The sheriff ran his hand through his silver hair. He arched his gray bushy eyebrows.

Colton shook his head. "No, just thinking you might want to make some improvements to this here buildin'."

The sheriff picked up the bag, jiggling it in his hand. "This'll pay for more than just improvements."

Colton stared him down. Most sheriffs in the West were crooked as the Mississippi. This sheriff didn't seem to be any different. "Do we have a deal?"

The sheriff shoved the small sack in his pocket. "Deal."

Colton waved toward Jace. "Come on out of there."

With a chuckle, Jace swung open the door to the jail cell.

The sheriff stood up straight. "What in the hell?"

"My brother has a talent for cracking locks." Colton waited for Jace to step out of the cell to join them.

Jace tipped his hat toward the sheriff. "Pleasure stayin' with you."

Red crept up the sheriff's face. "If you could do that the whole time, why'd you sit here?"

"Can't say. Could be those wanted posters don't do me justice. The likeness damn near never captures me right." Jace walked over to the wall where his gun belt hung. He pulled it around his waist. "Plus, I've been enjoyin' the company."

Jace and the sheriff turned in unison to look into the other cell. Colton followed their stares to where a small raven-haired beauty sat stiff as a board on the edge of the cot. She crossed her arms and raised her chin. With her shoulders squared, she looked past all of them like they didn't exist. Her heart-shaped face held delicate features that drew him in, capturing his attention. Her dusty pink lips looked as soft as satin, yet they sat in a firm line across her face. As he studied her, he couldn't help but wonder what her lips would feel like under his. Would the hard exterior she showed them melt away under his touch? Something in the way she narrowed her emerald eyes at him made him think she knew *exactly* what he was thinking.

Colton smacked the back of his hand against Jace's arm. "How'd she find herself in here?"

She tilted her head at him and crossed her arms. "Not sure that's any of your business."

Jace chuckled low in his throat. "Now that has been a point of contention."

"Whatever it was couldn't warrant a slip of thing like her to be in here." Colton took a step closer to the cells. Damned if he didn't want to pry open the bars and set her free. A woman like this would burn the both of them up from the inside out. His fingers twitched with the need to reach out and touch her cheek.

"This slip of a thing can take care of herself, thank you very much." She arched her eyebrow.

Jace caught Colton by the arm. "I wouldn't, if were you."

Colton stared down at Jace's hand. "Move it, or I'll move it for you."

Jace lifted his hand and chuckled. "Haven't gotten past that I see."

Colton shrugged but didn't answer. He preferred when people kept to themselves. With his eyes locked on the little hellion, he could tell by the hard set of her soft jawline she'd hand any man his balls. Her raven hair hung in knots down her back, yet she sat like a queen on a throne, rather than a criminal on a bedroll. Though her dress hung in tatters and was covered in grime, Colton could tell by the intricate details it was made of fine material. Not the type of thing a brothel worker could manage to purchase. He turned to the sheriff. "Ain't right seeing a lady in here."

"Then maybe you should bust me out." She arched her eyebrow, teasing him.

Jace let go of a low chuckle. "See, I told you to be careful."

The sheriff motioned toward her. "I'm not letting a woman like *that* loose on this town."

"Excuse me, I don't think I like what you're implying." She pursed her lips.

"Then I guess it's your lucky day. I'm not asking you, I'm telling you." Colton crossed his arms over his chest. He didn't know what he was doing, but he'd be damned if he sat by and watched a lady be harmed. Especially this one. With her dark good looks and fiery attitude, she'd be a hell of a challenge for him… and he loved a challenge.

"I'd say once he makes up his mind, that's all there is to it." Jace stared at the sheriff, then shifted his weight back on his heels and turned toward Colton. "Might want to make sure you know what you're doing. She's had a lot of suitors over the past few days, even when she didn't want them."

A light sigh drifted from her cell. "I didn't see you doing anything to stop them."

White hot anger flared through Colton. He turned on Jace, grabbing a fistful of his shirt. He shoved Jace backward, slamming him into the wall. "You stand by letting a woman endure those kinds of attentions?" Colton fought the urge to punch him. The sheriff shuffled uncomfortably, yet kept his distance.

Jace flashed his teeth in a humorless smile. They were nose to nose, and he spoke through his teeth. "Remember, I was there, too, when it happened. I'd never do her memory that kind of disrespect. I said the lady had a lot of suitors. I didn't say they got what they came for."

Colton took a step back, letting Jace's shirt go. His breath heaved in and out as flashes of his mother's death ran through his mind. The first wave of summer had settled over their home when Comanches attacked. Colton was no more than fourteen. His father had gotten off easy with a quick knife to the throat. But his mother, his poor mother, had been tortured for days. He, along with his six younger brothers, had been hog tied and left for dead. All the while, he watched as man after man ravaged his mother. At times, the younger ones dozed off, but not Colton. He'd locked his eyes on her, though she wouldn't look at him. He hadn't wanted her to go through it alone. It went on for days until the life had drained from those soft sapphire eyes. In his mind, any man who took to violating women deserved to find himself at the wrong end of Colton's knife, even if it was one of his brothers. "Lucky for you, they didn't."

Jace pushed Colton back. He stood with his fists at his sides. "I was raised better than that. You should know... *you* raised me."

"Then what the hell happened?" Colton stepped closer to the bars containing her.

She rolled her eyes. "What happened is I can take care of myself just fine."

"They went in with one intention. And came out eating their balls." Jace gave a humorless chuckle. "It was right entertaining to watch. At first, I thought I'd have to break us both out, but then she handled it. Didn't want a bounty on both of our heads. Thought that'd be bad."

A slow smile spread across her lush pouty lips as she rose from the bedroll and made her way to face Colton. Her slender hips swayed with every step she took towards him. The dark material of her dress swished against her legs. Four buttons at the top of her dress were missing, giving Colton the barest glimpse of pale, creamy skin. Attitude and beauty, there wasn't a deadlier combo. Like a punch to the gut, she floored him. She laced her fingers around the bars. "A bounty on my head wouldn't worry me." She shrugged. "There are far worse things in life."

"Shit, why didn't you say so? We could've been out of here days ago." Jace walked over the sheriff's rundown desk and hopped up on it.

The sheriff stepped in front of Colton, blocking his view of the woman. "I ain't takin' orders from you, *friend*. This here is what we call a grave digger. Ya see?"

Colton tilted his head to the side, looking around the sheriff. She stood a full head shorter than him, and looked to weigh as much as a bale of hay. "No. I don't see. What the hell were you doing when these suitors came to visit?"

The sheriff snapped his mouth shut. Jace slid off the desk and sauntered over to rest his elbow on the sheriff's shoulder. "The sheriff here is easily swayed by his pockets."

Colton looked him up and down. "Is that so? Well, here's a proposition for you." He bent down to the sheriff's level, getting in his face. "You can either do as I say, or I'll invite the rest of my kin for a visit."

Jace whistled. "Been a while since we came together."

"What'd you say your name was again?" The sheriff took a few steps back and leaned on his desk, studying his fingernails.

"Name's Colton Sutton. And what should I call you, Sheriff?" Colton offered him his hand.

The sheriff stood up straight and took his hand. "Sheriff Tully. You wouldn't be *the* Colton Sutton?"

"Do you know of any other Colton Suttons?" He turned to Jace with a half-smile.

The sheriff pointed toward Jace. "That'd make you Jace Sutton."

Jace tipped his hat. "The one and only."

"What do Satan's Sons want with our town?" Sheriff Tully murmured.

His raven-haired beauty sucked in a breath, her eyes rounded as she took a small step back. "Satan's Sons, holy hell."

"I'm no son of Satan. My momma was a saint!" Colton rested his hand on his gun. It wasn't a name he liked for his family. But after damn near dying at the age of fourteen, Colton had somehow managed to keep himself and his wily brothers alive long enough for them to grow into the men they were now. Colton had spent the better part of his twenties hunting down the men who'd terrorized his momma, bathing the southern territory in Comanche blood. They'd gained a reputation for burning a swathe through Texas and had been deemed Satan's Sons, because only the spawn of the devil could kill mercilessly. The world saw them as a hellish threat. If it kept the right people away, he'd live with it.

The sheriff held up his hands. "I didn't mean no offense. And I'm sure we can come to some kind of arrangement about the lady. Not sure if this town could survive your brothers. Is it true what they say about Luke?"

Colton brushed a hand over his chin. "What's that they say?"

Sheriff Tully's throat bobbed as he swallowed. "That he can call upon hellfire itself to do his bidding?"

Colton gave the sheriff a level look. "You lookin' to find out?"

He shook his head, his chubby jowls shaking with the movement. "No, no. I'll put her under your custody."

"You can't do that." She crossed her arms over her chest and stomped her foot.

The sheriff hiked up his pants. "I'll do whatever I damn well please, missy." He turned to Colton. "How long are you planning on stayin', Mr. Sutton?"

"Just until our business with Robert Buckley is complete." Colton turned back to the woman. She was some kind of temptress. With those emerald eyes looking up at him and her sassy ways, he swore she could get him to do anything.

When the sheriff didn't say anything, he turned to find the sheriff and Jace sharing a look. Colton bounced a glance between the two of them. "What aren't you telling me?"

The sheriff stuck his key into the cell door and turned to open it. "This here is Lily Buckley... Robert Buckley's wife."

Lily was anything but a delicate flower. With her dark looks, sashaying hips and too smart eyes, she was more like a raven on the hunt... *his raven.* She stepped out of the cell and faced Colton. He never took his eyes off her as he offered her his hand. "Pleased to meet you, ma'am. Why hasn't your husband come to fetch you?"

She placed her hand in his, her straight white teeth flashing when she broke into a smile. Like the cat who ate the mouse, she stood before him not batting an eyelash. "Haven't you heard, Mr. Colton? They say I killed my husband."

Colton's Ambush

Chapter 2

"Where you camped?" Colton asked Jace while stomping down the street back towards Scorpion, with Jace next to him and Lily following close behind.

"I had a room at the saloon." Jace glanced back toward Lily. "It's not the kind of place a respectable woman should go."

Colton nodded. "I think I figured that out for myself. I say we camp on the outskirts of town. Then head back in tomorrow to set things right."

"I'd think it would go against your constitution to make a lady like her sleep on the ground. There's not much to her. The cold alone could kill her." Jace sighed.

"I agree with Jace. You could let me go, and I'll be out of your hair." She looked up at him, her eyes full of hope.

Colton looked back at her. The sheriff had insisted on keeping her hands tied, yet Colton thought animals got more respect than his raven. She followed behind him, watching him the way a doctor studies books. When their eyes locked, she stiffened and lifted her chin. Colton shrugged. "Can't let you go. This here's Comanche territory. You'll end up dead within a week."

"I've survived worse," she sighed.

"Such as?" He crossed his arms waiting for her to speak, yet she held her tongue.

"I think we should find a respectable establishment," Jace interrupted, breaking the silence between them.

Colton looked up and down the street. "I don't think there is one. I reckon we bundle her up real good. Plant her next to a fire."

"And after that?" Jace stopped in the middle of the road. The sun had set, leaving only the light from the oil lamps in the saloon to illuminate the street.

"What do you mean?" Colton faced him.

"You can't just keep her. She's not a stray dog. It's indecent. Unless you intend on marrying?"

Lily scoffed. "I do believe I have a choice in this, and the answer is no."

Colton looked at her sideways. "I'm on the wrong side of thirty-five. If there ain't a chain around my ankle by now, there ain't going to be one." Though truth be told, when he looked at Lily, matrimony didn't seem too awful. The thought of coming home to her every night, with her midnight locks spread across his pillow, made him feel like it might not be so bad. Colton glanced back at her, once again locking his eyes with hers. An odd feeling overcame him. Why couldn't he marry her? "Hey, why'd you immediately say no?"

"Because you're a Sutton. And I had enough bad husbands to last me a lifetime." She waved away the question.

"What makes you think I can't fulfill my husbandly duties?" She definitely had a way of making him raise his hackles. Damned if it wasn't sexy as all get out.

She crossed her arms over her chest. "What makes you think you can?"

"Raven, I'm good at what I set my mind to." He winked at her.

"You're scandalous."

"Only if you're lucky." He smirked down at her.

"Grab the reins! Get 'em! Hold him still." Shouts drifted down the street toward them, pulling Colton back from his thoughts of Lily.

Jace snickered. "Scorpion?"

"Bastards deserve what they get." Colton shrugged while they lumbered toward the saloon and the post where he'd tacked Scorpion.

As they got closer, Colton saw Scorpion rear up in the middle of the town, his reins hanging loose, swinging around, while he kicked his front legs. Men swarmed around him, circling him in an attempt to trap him. Jace stopped just outside of the stream of light coming from the saloon, keeping to the shadows. Colton stood by his side, and from behind him he heard a light huff. "Something funny?"

Her voice came out as sultry as the rest of her. "I hope the beast stomps them all." The West could be a cruel place with cruel, hard people. As Colton studied her heart-shaped face for any signs of concern for the men, he found her lips pressed into a hard line. Her eyebrows drew tight over her emerald eyes while she watched the scene without a sign of concern.

Just then, Scorpion spun in a circle and bucked his back legs, kicking two men square in their chests and sending them flying. Jace smacked the back of his hand against Colton's arm while he hunched over laughing. "Can't decide what they know less about, horses or cards."

Jace had always been the joker of the family. Some would call him a thief, others a gambler, or even a ladies' man. But to the Sutton family, he remained the joker. With an easy smile, he favored his mother's good looks and his father's temperament. Colton was the complete opposite. With his dark eyes and stoic personality, he had a reputation for being the coldest, meanest brother and leader of the Sutton boys. Colton envied Jace's ability to forget the past. For other members of the family, it had left wounds that had yet to heal, especially for Colton and the second eldest, Luke. Hell, his wounds were visible on the outside. They were old enough for the memories to be branded into their minds. "Is that how you ended up in jail? Cards?"

Jace nodded with a crooked smile. "Among other things."

"I don't want to know about other things." Colton stepped forward, about to enter the circle of men, when a small hand grabbed his elbow. He froze mid-step, not hating the sensation of her touch, which was a surprise to him.

She stepped up beside him. "You can't go in there."

"Afraid I'll get trampled?" He looked down at her hand but allowed it to stay there.

Lily dug her fingers into his arm. "You die, and I go back to that cell."

"And here I thought you were sweet on me." He bent over and placed a light kiss on her cheek. She gasped and raised her eyebrows at him. With a chuckle, he stepped out of her hold. "Keep an eye on her," he directed Jace.

He moved closer to Scorpion. The damn horse flung itself around in a full rage. He bucked and reared like he'd been bitten by a snake. His eyes wide with excitement, he blew hard puffs of air from his nose. Foam gathered around the bit in his mouth, and with each toss of his head, saliva flew in all directions. He stomped the ground, sending up pieces of dirt and rock.

When Colton stepped into the circle of men, he tipped his hat at the gunslinger and his compadres who were all standing side by side with their hands out. "Any particular reason y'all riled up my animal?"

"We didn't rile him. He damn near took a chunk out of my horse. We's just movin' him." The slinger stood before him covered in sweat, with his hat and jacket missing.

"Uh-huh. Movin' him where?" Colton pulled out a hand-rolled and lit the end. A man ran straight at Scorpion and jumped onto his back, trying to swing his leg up into the saddle. The others piped up in a chorus of cheers. Colton crossed his arms over his chest, watching as Scorpion's eyes rounded, his ears pressed flat against his head. The horse' muscles bunched and he shot straight up in the air. All four of his hooves flew off the ground. He spun midair and landed on his side crushing the man clinging to the saddle.

From behind him, he heard a gasp escape Lily's lips. "Hellfire runs in that animal's veins!"

Colton took a deep drag of his cigarette and let smoke drift from his mouth. He tossed it to the side. "Then only the devil can tame him." Colton stepped into the ring, facing off against Scorpion. He gave a low, drawn-out whistle.

Scorpion rose up onto all fours, his tail still swishing. He clomped the ground around him but seemed to be reining in his temper. His breath evened out, he stopped bucking, and his head dropped just a bit lower. Colton took a step forward. "Easy, Scor, easy." The horse swung towards him like he was going to trample him. Colton never flinched. Instead, he reached out and placed a calloused hand on the horse's flanks. The muscles under Colton's touch twitched, yet Scorpion remained steady. Even at just over six feet tall, Colton was dwarfed by Scorpion. No matter the size difference, they were made for each other. There was a saying: "Like owner, like animal," and the two of them matched each other in both temperament and looks. Scorpion's chestnut hair was only a shade darker than Colton's, and though Scorpion had big brown eyes, Colton's were a lighter dusty brown. Scor was family to Colton. In his eye, disrespecting his horse was like an insult to him.

"Someone rope him," one of the men called.

Jace moved next to the man in an instant. "You're a damn fool." The cock of a pistol brought the crowd up short.

Colton knew it was Jace holding the gun by the familiar sound it made. "Brother, you plannin' on shooting someone?"

"It's a consideration."

"Well, don't hit my horse." Colton trusted Jace with his life and knew from experience he was a dead shot. In the West, all a man had was himself, his horse, and maybe—if he was as lucky as Colton—he had a strong family around him.

"Wouldn't dream of it," Jace chuckled.

Scorpion turned his head toward Colton, bumping him with his nose. Colton opened his hand and ran it between his beast's eyes. "That a boy."

He grabbed the reins and led Scorpion back toward Lily. She took a tentative step back but held her ground and lifted her chin. He shook his head. "He ain't gonna hurt you."

"Who said it was the horse I was worried about?" She held her hand in front of her. If he didn't know they were tied together, he would've thought she just clasped them in front of her.

"Well, saddle up, sweetheart." He came up beside her and leaned in, whispering in her ear. "It's going to be a bumpy ride. I've a hankering for a full belly and some shuteye. But with you around, I don't think I'll be sleeping much."

Her eyes widened as she pressed her lips into a hard line. She tossed her hair over her shoulder and held up her chin in that proud way she had about her. "I'm not sleeping near you."

"Raven, you'll sleep where I tell you to. I done busted you out of jail, and this here territory ain't safe." He patted Scorpion's nose. "You stay, boy."

The crowd of men began to gather, watching the interchange between them. The gunslinger strolled to the front of the pack. "Well, look what we got here." In the time it took for Colton to calm Scorpion the slinger had found his hat. He tipped it at Lily. "Lily, so good to see you not behind bars."

She turned her face away from him and mumbled, "Clint."

"Don't get all shy on me now. You were much louder the other night." The men around them sniggered. A red flush crept up Lily's face. Her eyes rounded with shock, but she pressed her lips together, not saying a word.

Jace holstered his gun and stepped in front of the man. "You know, I do believe you're right, *Clint.*" He hissed his name like a curse. "I seem to remember some screaming the night you came to her cell like a snake in the grass. 'Cept the screaming wasn't her. How'd your balls taste after she fed 'em to you?"

Clint shoved Jace, but Jace, being the stubborn bastard Colton raised him to be, didn't move.

The two men stood nose to nose as Clint poked a finger into Jace's chest. "Y'all must be crazy in the head." He pointed to his temple. "Don't you know who you're messing with?"

"Can't say that I do. Why don't you introduce yourself properly... *friend.*" Jace bumped him back with his chest.

Clint rested his hand on his belt just next to his gun. "Y'all are outnumbered."

Jace looked back at Colton with a shrug. "The odds appear to be in our favor. What do you think, Colton?"

Colton motioned to the two men standing closest to him. "I'd give these two a head start… just to make it fair."

Colton stepped up next to Jace and pulled him back. "I'll handle this."

Before Jace took a full step back, Colton lunged forward and slung his fist across Clint's face. Clint's head snapped back. He stumbled, falling into the men standing behind him. They pushed him forward back into the fray. Colton caught him by the collar of his jacket and shook him. "A man should know how to treat a lady." He hauled his fist back again and let it fly across Clint's face, knocking him square in the nose. Blood poured down Clint's mouth and chin, coating his lips in a river of crimson.

Clint's two friends jumped into the mix and grabbed Colton's arms, pulling him away from Clint, restraining him. Jace ran at Clint, knocking him to the side with a tackle, while Colton struggled against the men holding him. They pulled at his arms, spreading them out widely, like they were holding him up to take a beating. Two other men jumped on top of Jace, pulling him off Clint. The two brothers looked at each other while both were being held. Clint staggered to his feet, wiped the blood from his mouth and took shaky steps towards Colton. "You should know who you're dealing with, boy."

Colton flat out laughed. Even though he was restrained and could barely move, he chuckled in the face of a fight. "Perhaps you should ask yourself the same thing."

Colton leaned his weight into the men holding him and kicked out his legs, connecting with Clint's chest, sending him flying backward into the group holding Jace. They fell to the ground in a pile of flailing limbs. Colton shoved out his arm, knocking one of his captors away long enough to swing around and slug the other one in the temple. Colton gave a humorless laugh as the man slumped to the ground listlessly. He took a step forward about to check to see if the man was still alive when another slinger jumped on his back. With cat-like reflexes, he threw his weight forward, bent over and flipped the man over his back and straight onto the ground.

Dust kicked up into his eyes, yet he never blinked as he kicked the guy in the ribs. He was about to kick him a second time, when a gunshot rang out, freezing everyone in place. Colton turned to find Sheriff Tully standing with his shotgun pointed in the air. "Y'all better knock this racket off before I start putting holes in ya."

Colton took a deep breath. "Won't be necessary, Sheriff. Jace and I was just leavin'."

The sheriff nodded toward the edge of town. "Best get a move on then."

Jace ambled to Colton's side with a shit-eating grin on his face. "Quite the tussle."

"That it was." Colton nodded and turned back toward Lily who stood holding Scorpion's reins. The horse pressed his nose to her shoulder, allowing Lily to pet him. Colton tapped Jace's arm and pointed toward Lily. "Would you look at that."

"I'll be damned. That horse never lets anyone but you touch him." Jace clapped Colton on the shoulder as he walked over to her.

Clint stumbled in front of them, blocking them from getting to Lily. "Who the hell are you?"

Jace held out his hand like nothing had happened. "Jason Sutton." He motioned to Colton. "This here's my brother, Colton."

He didn't take Jace's offered hand. He stood holding his arm across his stomach like he'd gotten punched in the bread basket a little too hard. "As in… Satan's Sons?"

Colton gritted his teeth and took a step closer. Though the name never sat right, he owned it. He nodded. "Because only the devil himself could father sons like us."

The rowdy group took a collective step back, looking as though they'd all seen better days. Colton took a deep breath, the throbbing in his hand subsiding with each passing moment. Though he'd been the center of his tussle, he felt none the worse for wear. When he reached Lily's side, he smiled down at her. "Hold Scorpion for just a bit longer?"

She looked up at him with wide eyes filled with fear. Yet she met his challenge head on and narrowed those beautiful emerald eyes at him while she held the leather lead. Colton stepped up next to Jace and placed his hand on his gun. "What'll it be, boys? You gonna stop me from being on my way?"

Clint took a larger step backward. "Not today, Sutton. Not today." His words held a promise of retribution tomorrow.

Colton motioned to the men around them. "Good. Then best be movin' on."

"I'll be seeing you, Sutton." Clint looked Lily up and down while licking his bloody lips. "You too, Ms. Lily."

The crowd around them drifted away, and the three of them were alone, standing in the darkness once again. "Best be finding a safe spot to bed down."

"I've been thinking on it." Jace looked back at Lily. "Buckley ranch is in debt to us. We've paid enough into it to claim some ownership. With Robert Buckley dead, could be a nice piece of dirt to hold."

Colton nodded. "Not a bad thought."

"My home does not belong to you!" Lily interrupted.

"Well, your husband owes us damn near two thousand gold pieces. How you plan on repaying his debt?"

She stepped up to Colton, looking him dead in the eye. "I don't like your tone."

Colton did all he could to suppress his smile. Nothing got to him better than a woman with fire in her belly. "Then I suggest you get used to it."

She held her bound hands in his face. "What do you want with me?"

"Haven't decided yet, ma'am."

In truth, he had no idea why he needed to keep her close, but something in him wanted her near him. With her dark mane, vibrant eyes, and curvy body, he could get used to having her around. Add in her fiery temper, and she was a recipe that could fill his belly.

"I'm no whore." She took a deep breath. "Best keep your hands to yourself."

Under the smell of horse and dirt, he could make out the faintest hit of honeysuckle. When Colton raised his hand to straighten his hat, Lily flinched back. She threw up her arms to cover her face. Colton and Jace cursed under their breath. For all the iciness she'd shown him, Lily Buckley had her own set of ugly secrets. She peeked up at him from under her arm. At her own pace, she stood up, meeting his eyes.

Colton nodded to her. "I'll keep that in mind."

"I hate to break up this little party, but we best be goin'." Jace grabbed Scorpion's reins and led him down the street.

"Lead the way." Colton waved his arm allowing Lily to pass in front of him.

Lily took five steps past him then turned to look at him over her shoulder. "Before it was Buckley ranch, it was Montero property. Which makes it mine."

"Who's Montero?" Colton called to her.

"My father, God rest his soul." She turned away, sashaying into the night.

Colton's Ambush

Chapter 3

After being married to Robert Buckley for three long, horrible years, sitting in jail for two weeks had been a reprieve from hell. Despite all the trials she'd endured, they were nothing in comparison to the life she'd led. But standing face to face with Colton Sutton could very well be the end of her. Watching him stand against a town full of less-than-reputable men and then the hellion of a horse, she couldn't decide if crazy ran in his family or if he wore his bravery like a second skin. At the moment, crazy seemed to be more likely. She could feel his eyes watching her every move, like a predator on the prowl.

The rough bindings at her wrist bit into her skin. Try as she might, they wouldn't loosen. Lily tilted back her head and walked into the night with two of the scariest men she'd ever come in contact with following her home. A rough hand ran down her arm and stopped at her wrist. She jumped back, pulling her hands away from Colton, her heart up in her throat. Though his touch was gentle, it came as a surprise to her.

Colton stood a hair's width taller than Jace, yet both towered over her. But it wasn't his size that scared her. The way he looked at her with those desert-colored eyes made her nerves stand on edge. It was as though he saw right through her walls into her soul. His angular jaw jutted out each time she surprised him, and though dirt and grime covered him from head to toe, she saw the handsome man hidden underneath. If the ladies didn't come calling for Colton Sutton now, there was no doubt in Lily's mind it would happen soon. This was the type of man every Western woman desired—someone who could protect their home, children and life. If one of Satan's Sons couldn't do it, then no one could.

He held up his hands where she could see them. "Easy there." He used the same tone with her as he had with his wild horse. It lulled her into a sense of calmness she hadn't felt in years.

She took a small step back. "Just because I'm in your custody doesn't mean you own me."

"I'll keep that in mind." His drawl did things to her she didn't care to admit. But when he looked down at her from under the brim of his hat, she felt lost in a sea of his eyes. He took a step closer. "If I cut those ropes, you gonna run?"

She shook her head, unable to form words past the ball of excitement in her throat. Not being restrained by bars or ropes had her shaking in anticipation. Colton slid an ugly looking knife from behind his back. It had a shining, jagged blade the size of her forearm. Lily turned her head away and held out her hands. If the knife slipped and nicked her skin, she didn't want to see the blood. Colton drew the blade over the ropes, allowing them to fall to the ground in tatters. She rubbed at her wrists. "Thank you."

"Anyone ever tell you, you got a way of making gratitude sound like a curse?" He slid the knife behind his back and out of sight.

"No." She turned from him and continued to walk into the night.

They were just at the edge of town when the clomping of hooves warned her only moments before her feet left the ground and she found herself planted firmly in Colton's lap. The saddle creaked under the weight of the two of them as she gasped in shock. How had he mounted Scorpion so fast and picked her up as though she weighed nothing? She kicked her legs, trying to squirm out of his grip. Scorpion side-stepped in protest of the violent movements. Colton wound his arm tighter around her waist and pulled in the reins. "You want to get thrown? Settle down."

She hesitated a fraction of a second. When she felt him pressing into her backside through her dress, she threw her arms and legs around, objecting fiercely. Colton barely held the reins while Scorpion began prancing nervously. "Stop it. You kicked him!"

Lily froze, her heart racing, her breath heaving in and out. The cool night air did nothing to calm her. "I am sorry. You startled me."

Colton looked to Jace and nodded his head. "Be seeing you shortly."

"Wait," she said. "You can't just leave him here." What was she saying? She had a better chance of getting away with only one of them around. But being alone with Colton worried her. The man had a way of calming and exciting her all at once.

"Oh, don't you go worrying your pretty little head about me. I see me some good horse meat." Jace tilted his head toward the horses hitched to the post outside the saloon.

"You can't." Lily wiggled against Colton. He didn't move or try to stop her. He held her against him just tightly enough to keep her still. She didn't particularly care if Jace stole the horses from the men in that saloon—hell, half of them had tried to sully her in the jail cell—but she didn't want Jace bringing trouble to her doorstep by stealing those animals. She had enough of fiendish men to last her a lifetime.

"Why not? They were set on taking Scorpion." Colton shrugged, then squeezed his legs, urging Scorpion forward and leaving Jace to acquire some new animals.

Lily bounced in Colton's lap as Scorpion headed out of town at a steady gait. She gritted her teeth. "I can feel you pressing into me."

"You're a beautiful woman, Raven," he whispered as though he'd answered her accusation.

She shoved her elbow back into his gut, yet he barely flinched. A light throbbing started in her arm from smacking into the hard planes of his stomach, yet she refused to rub at it. "Why do you call me that?"

"Seems fittin'." He pushed Scorpion into a gallop. "You don't talk like you're from around here."

"I was raised back East."

"You got any kinfolk there now?"

She shrugged. "My uncle is still there, I think."

"Maybe you should return home? The West ain't no place for gentlewomen." His breath drifted in light puffs across her ear.

"I am home." She spoke through clenched teeth.

"Home is where ever you make it, Raven."

Lily closed her mouth as they rode out of town and toward the Buckley ranch. She tilted back her head, looking up at the stars glimmering down on them. The full moon hung low in the sky, illuminating the land around them, painting the rough landscape in shades of moonlit blues and purples. For a moment, she closed her eyes, wishing she could escape the hell her life had become. Her insides were a mess of nerves. With Colton, she didn't know what to expect. Would he hurt her, or would he hold his manhood in check? At least she knew what to expect of her now-deceased husband. She couldn't decide which was better—the devil you know or the devil you don't.

The ride from town to Buckley Ranch was a straight shot, filled with flat land and a rocky mountain range in the distance. On a hot summer day, heat seeped into the hard-packed ground, making it feel like burning stone under her feet rather than desert sand. But at this time of night, the temperature dropped until the chill seeped deep into her bones. She fought against the shiver that overtook her body. Colton pulled his jacket around them, surrounding her in the heat coming off his body. Neither of them spoke as he tucked her in closer to him. Lily would never admit it, but at that moment, she was happy to have his warmth surrounding her.

Buckley Ranch seemed to come upon them faster than she'd thought. Once, it'd been a place she'd called home; but when her bastard of a husband took over, it had become a place she associated with pain. The land around the ranch stretched for miles. In the distance, a sheer cliff rose up behind the ranch, protecting it from intruders. It faced the town so anyone who approached could be spotted easily. In the past, her mother would've kept a light burning in the window, but now the large wood-planked house stood completely dark, looking as though the love had left its walls long ago.

The front door stood dead center of the exterior wall, with a small porch running the length of the house. An overhang protected the porch from the midday sun. As a child, Lily loved to sit in the rockers and watch her father training horses in the pen off to the side. Her mother would peek out the window and hand Lily bits of bread and treats as she watched him all afternoon.

Colton grabbed her arm, bringing her back to the present. "Slide on down."

Lily clung to Colton's arm as she let her body slide off Scorpion. The horse was massive, and even hanging from Colton she still didn't feel the ground under her feet. She panicked and dug her nails into his skin as she swung her legs, searching for her footing. She squeezed her eyes shut, praying she wouldn't get thrown or fall from Scorpion. Broken bones were not something she wanted to relive. Scorpion shifted, protesting her dangling off his back like a wet blanket. She squealed and tried to pull herself back up.

Colton's hand wrapped around her forearm like a lifeline. "Lily, look at me." She peeked up at him. His face reflected the light of the moon making his eyes hypnotic. She instantly calmed under his steady gaze. She took a deep breath and stopped flailing. "You're just a little hop off the ground. I'm gonna ease you on down."

Lily nodded. Her hair fell into her face, but she didn't dare let go of Colton's arm. Cool air brushed her legs as she slid from the horse. When her toes touched the ground, Colton let her arm drop. She tilted forward, trying to catch her balance as she waved her arms. Then somehow, she spun around and fell face first into Scorpion's side. She reached out and grabbed hold of Colton's thigh, finding her balance. She pulled back her hands and straightened her skirts. "Anyone ever tell you it's not polite to throw women off horses, especially hellion horses?"

As if he understood, Scorpion stomped his hoof and chuffed. Colton swung his leg over Scorpion's neck and slid down like he'd done it all his life. He pulled the reins over his head. "Can't say I know any hellion horses."

She crossed her arms. "Contrary man."

"I'll own up to that." He stepped in closer to her.

Lily tried to take a step back, but she didn't move fast enough. Colton wrapped his arms around her, pressing his body into hers. She braced for the worst, but he made no move to throw her to the ground. She froze, teetering between fighting him off or exploring the way he made her feel.

He shook his head as if he knew her thoughts. He ran his hand down her cheek. Though his skin held the roughness of a working man, his touch was gentler than she'd ever felt. "Easy. I ain't gonna hurt you."

"That's what all men say, then you find yourself on your back with no place to go." She squirmed in his arms, yet he didn't let go. Panicked, she pushed at his chest. She'd been deceived by men before. This time she knew what to expect. Colton Sutton could be as tender as he wanted. She wasn't falling for it.

"I'm sorry you lived through that, Raven. But ain't no one gonna hurt you now. Not unless they want their lives cut short."

She stopped struggling against him. When she looked up into his eyes, she felt as though he would melt her on the spot. Slower than a lazy river, he leaned into her and pressed his lips to hers, his kiss surprisingly tender but firm. He held himself there as though waiting for her to give in. His arms drifted up her back around her shoulders, wrapping her in a cocoon of warmth. Her mind screamed for her to knee him in the balls and run, but her body begged him for more. She pressed her lips to his, melding them to his mouth. When he dipped his tongue between her lips, she gasped but opened farther, allowing her tongue to dance with his. Never before had a man kissed her the way Colton did. Being around him was a whirlwind of emotions she didn't know how to handle. One minute, she wanted to run. The next, she wanted to stay. Only one thing was for sure... Colton Sutton was a danger to her heart.

With a sigh, she rested her hands on his chest, letting him hold her. They explored each other while their lips melded together. Heat bloomed between them, and Lily found herself melting for him.

Colton broke the kiss and chuckled against her lips. "You're gonna burn us both up, Raven."

Lily pulled back like she'd been doused with water. What the hell was she doing? This was Colton Sutton, one of Satan's Sons. He didn't get a reputation like his for nothing. Regaining her senses, she put her hands on her hips. "No."

"No?" Colton pulled off his hat, allowing his dark hair to fall into his eyes.

When he lifted his arm, Lily took a step back, covering her face from the blow she knew was about to come. In her experience, men who got denied became violent, and the best thing she could do was save her face from being bruised up. There was nothing worse than people staring at you over a purple eye. She closed her eyes. "Go ahead and hit me. I give as good as I get!" she threatened from under her arm. He would wear himself out, then she'd get her revenge.

"I just bet you do." Colton's words hit her in calm, steady waves. She lowered her arms, peeking up at him. He stood watching her, always weighing and measuring like he was taking stock of her. "I ain't in the habit of striking a woman for sayin' no."

"You'd be the first man I met who didn't." She crossed her arms.

He shrugged. "Honey is sweeter when it's given." He reached over and wrapped his hand around hers, tugging her lightly toward the side of the house, where they would be hidden in the shadows.

Lily followed behind him. When he reached the wall, he turned and pressed her up against it. "I'm not gonna hurt you, I promise. A man deserves to prove himself based on his own doings, not the doings of others." He dusted her neck with a feather-light kiss.

She arched back, tilting her head, allowing him to get closer. He ran his tongue over her skin, leaving a trail of moisture on her neck. She leaned back with a moan. Never before had a man taken the time to make sure she felt good. His hands trailed up her body, pushing inside her dress. The tip of his finger danced across her taught nipple. Lily cried out, clutching to him.

"I knew you'd be like this," he whispered in her ear. He then pressed a light kiss to her neck. "Raven, you're gonna be the death of me."

Heat rose over her skin. It was the first time any man had made her crave more. Her hands drifted over his arms and up to his shoulders. She needed him closer. Would Colton Sutton be the man he said he was? He seemed too good to be true with his good looks, strong character and domineering ways. A man like this could have a woman falling for him in no time. But would she be another broken heart lying in the dust? Her heart raced at the thought of being loved by Colton. But was he capable of it?

The clomping of hooves signaled the arrival of Jace. She took a deep breath and squirmed away from Colton. Getting a reprieve from him and the extreme effects he had on her would be a blessing. Colton grabbed her just above her elbow and guided her out in front of the house to meet Jace.

Jace stopped a few feet in front of them. He ran his eyes over Lily. Heat rose in her cheeks, but she held her tongue. Would Jace know what they'd just been doing? He slid off the horse with all the grace in the world. "Damn, girl, your rear must be screaming after bouncing on that horse all this way." He pulled his hat off. "I was watching as y'all took off."

Lily gave him a tight smile, and held her chin up the way her mother taught her to do anytime she felt embarrassed. "No, I'm fine." She pulled her arm away from Colton's grip.

"Your husband never taught you to ride?" Jace banged out his hat on his thigh.

"My husband taught me a lot of things… Riding wasn't one of them." She stormed toward her home, wanting to put as much distance between her and Colton as possible.

Colton's Ambush

Chapter 4

Riding wasn't one of them. Her words echoed in Colton's head all night long. One could only imagine what a man like Robert Buckley had taught his too young, too pretty wife. It led Colton to have a lot of questions. He didn't believe Lily had the guts to kill a man. She was tough, would hand them their balls on a platter, but to label her as a killer didn't fit. Looking at her face when she'd mentioned the things she'd learned had him doubting himself. Her nose had wrinkled in disgust and she wrapped her arms around herself, like she'd needed the comfort. The picture of her in his head kept him up damn near all night. He tossed around, pondering Lily and all the things she might've been through, until finally just before dawn he decided the shuteye he needed wasn't coming.

The quiet of the house surrounded him as the sun rose above the horizon. He sat in the small kitchen, waiting for his coffee to brew. Last night had been interesting. Lily had stormed into the house and pointed out each of the bedrooms. While there were three good options of rooms with lavish furnishings, comfortable beds and windows overlooking the property, he noticed Lily didn't choose a single one. Instead, she barricaded herself into a back bedroom with no windows, a small bed and nothing on the walls. It suited Colton just fine. If she insisted on being in a room like that with no way in or out, he'd go right ahead and let her.

Jace ambled into the kitchen, looking like the wrong side of a dog. His hair stood at attention, and he rubbed at the beard covering his face. "Coffee?"

"Just about done." Colton kicked out a chair from under the table and motioned for Jace to sit.

Jace slouched into the chair, yawning as he went down. He'd spent the night sleeping in a chair in the hall, ensuring Lily didn't make a run for it. A woman like her would never survive alone in the desert, yet he felt she'd try to do just that. Colton leaned his elbows on the table. "What happened in that jail?"

Jace ran his hand over the back of his neck. "You mean with her?" He motioned down the hall.

Colton nodded. It looked to him like Lily had seen better days. A woman with beauty like hers didn't learn to fight with fire in her veins for no reason. "She's got a bit of sass to her."

Jace arched his eyebrows. "You can say that again. But I suppose a woman in her position would be something like a cornered rat."

"You think she killed Robert Buckley?" Colton rose, walked over to the stove and poured them two cups of coffee. Steam drifted up from the tin cups, the smell of fresh coffee perfuming the air around him. He walked back over to the small table and handed Jace the cup of steaming goodness.

Jace shrugged. "Robert Buckley was a mean son of a bitch. No doubt he deserved what he got. But it's hard to say if he was murdered."

42

Colton sat up straight. "Was he shot?"

"I heard it was either poison or an attack of the heart." Jace shook his head. "Damn awful way to go."

"Poison is a woman's way of killin'. Men will shoot ya, hang ya, or just beat you down. But a woman is smart. She'll do it in such a way that no one will find out." Colton took a sip of his coffee allowing the liquid to warm him. In his wild days of riding across this land with his brothers at his side, he'd only come across a few women who mastered the art of killing with poison. But out of all those women, only one got him going. It was a hard way of life out West. He needed a hard woman. But at the same time, he needed a soft one who could stand at his side as a partner. His Raven seemed just the type.

As though his thoughts had conjured her, she walked in like it was a new day. Her hair was combed back from her face and tied into a long braid, which ran down the side of her body and bounced off her generous breasts. She inhaled deeply and closed her eyes. Those beautiful breasts popped at the top of her bust line. "Coffee."

"You're welcome to it. I tend to make it on the strong side," Colton warned.

"Of course, I'm welcome to it. This is *my* ranch." She breezed past him, bathing him in her honeysuckle scent.

Jace raised his eyebrows and slouched back in his chair with a chuckle. Colton watched as she moved around the kitchen with a familiarity only she would have. "I think the ownership of this ranch is a point we need to clarify." She stiffened for a moment but didn't say anything. Colton took a sip then set his cup back on the table. "Unless you plan on finding a way to work off the money this here property owes us, the way I see it, y'all are mortgaged to me. And I'm callin' it."

Lily spun on her heels with her eyes flaring wide. Any moment, her ears were gonna blow like a steam engine. She took a deep breath and spoke to him through gritted teeth. "This ranch was my father's, and it will be mine. I have a negotiation for you."

Colton leaned back in his chair and crossed his arms. "I'm listening."

*****

He had a way of looking at her that made her feel naked in front of a crowd and powerful all at the same time. It was as though every word she spoke he weighed, measured and found her wanting more out of life. She took a sip of her coffee, the hot goodness sliding down her throat, reminding her of how strong her mother used to make it.

"This is my land," she said firmly but gently. "It was given to me by my father. I'll let you use it as a pass-through for your cattle in exchange for protection guaranteed by Satan's Sons. You and your brothers can come and go as you need, so long as we have an understanding... I wish to be left alone."

In her twenty-six years of life, she'd known very little peace. Her home had always been a happy place for her until

Buckley showed up. If she could have some semblance of her life again, she might start to feel whole once more.

Jace chuckled but didn't speak. Instead, he looked at his big brother. Colton's lips twitched as if he were fighting a smile. He raised his cup to his mouth and took a deep drink. "I assume there is room for negotiation?"

Lily nodded and sat beside him, calmly waiting to hear what he had to say. Colton turned to Jace. "Mind giving us a minute."

With a nod of his head, Jace rose from his chair. "I'll check the horses." He left the room without a backward glance.

Colton stood, flipped his chair around and straddled it, then he grabbed her chair and pulled it in toward him. They were so close, the smell of tobacco, desert sun and man invaded her senses. Lily's knees skimmed the back of his chair and his inner thighs. She tried to pretend she didn't feel the tension between them and the heat flooding low in her stomach. But Colton Sutton had an irresistible charm she couldn't put her finger on. He crossed his arms over the back of the chair. "The way I see it, Raven, you've got some options, none of them you're gonna like."

"And what might those be?" She arched her eyebrow at him.

"Got company!" Jace yelled from out front.

Colton shot to his feet and wrapped his gun belt around his hips. "We'll have to continue this later."

The damn man had her flustered from head to toe. She thought, after washing up and feeling more human this morning, she could forget what'd happened between them last night and move forward. But here she sat with her hands shaking, her knees about to buckle and a slow heat building between her legs. She shoved herself up from her chair and stomped out the door into the early morning sun. She shielded her eyes with her hand, looking out toward the town. "Who is it?"

Jace and Colton stood side by side with their hands resting on their gun belts. Colton glanced over his shoulder at her. "Looks like Sheriff Tully with some company."

"You loaded?" Jace glanced down at Colton's gun.

Colton nodded while starting at the two men as they brought their horses to a stop in front of the house. Sheriff Tully stepped around his mount and headed straight for Colton. "Good mornin'."

Colton kicked at a rock beneath his foot. "That all depends on why you're here."

Lily's heart raced as she watched them move toward her. Were they here to take her back to jail? She took a small step back, wanting to disappear into the house. Colton reached behind him and pulled her closer to his side. "Ain't no one gonna come near you."

"Except you." She pulled her hand out of his. Why did he think he could just go about running things?

His lips twitched, but he didn't smile. "Except me."

The sheriff stopped short and turned to the man accompanying him. Lily could only make out his shadow. He wasn't a large man and looked to be wearing robes. "Father Morgan?"

"Hello, my child." Father Morgan extended his hand toward her. When she grasped it, he pulled her close and wrapped his arm around her, hugging her the way her father used to.

"Sheriff, what can I do you for?" Colton's stiff posture shifted in to a relaxed stance. He dropped his hand from his gunbelt.

"I got this here telegram from Daniel Buckley." Tully pulled a small piece of paper from his pocket and unfolded it. Lily sucked in a sharp breath. Many in the territory believed Robert Buckley to be the worst of the two Buckley brothers. They would be wrong. When it came to violence, Daniel Buckley made a study of torturing and killing people. Lily considered herself lucky having gotten settled with Robert, especially since Daniel had become a widower... three times.

"Forgive me, Sheriff, but what does Daniel Buckley have to do with anything?" Jace took a step closer.

The sheriff held his hands out in a stopping motion. "Well, now it's my job to notify the kin when someone dies. So I sent a telegram to him a few weeks back, letting him know his brother had passed on." He shot a hard glance at Lily. She stood up straight and held her head high. No use looking guilty when she wanted to be proven innocent. The sheriff shook his head. "Anyways, he just sent this to us this morning."

Lily held onto Father Morgan as she stood waiting to hear what Daniel had to say. She sent a silent prayer to the heavens, hoping he wouldn't come here. If he did, she would be dead for sure. One way or another, he would kill her. Jace snatched the paper out of the sheriff's hands. He unfolded it quickly and read it to himself.

"What's it say?" Colton pulled a hand-rolled from his pocket and lit it.

The smell of smoke and tobacco wafted toward Lily, calming her. Something about it reminded her of being wrapped in Colton's arms. She took a deep breath, waiting for Jace to tell her Daniel would be here soon... then she'd be a dead woman.

Jace shifted his weight from one foot to the other. "Well, it looks like we'll be expecting some visitors."

Colton took a deep drag before tossing the cigarette to the ground. After taking two large steps, he ripped the paper out Jace's hand. After reading it quickly, he crumpled it into his fist. "This here says he's coming to claim his brother's land for his own."

"What?" Lily's body shook with rage from head to toe. "He has no claim to the land. It is mine and mine alone!"

"Well, prepare yourself, Raven. He says, along with the land, he's coming to look after you."

All four men stared at her with pity in their eyes, their lips pressed into thin lines.

Colton turned toward the sheriff. "There is nothing you can do?"

Tully looked down at his feet. "I'm only one man, and we need to keep the peace."

"You figuring on hanging her? There's no proof she killed Robert Buckley. And my constitution goes against seeing a woman swing."

The sheriff shook his head. "Now, now. I can't say for sure if she killed Robert or not. No use dragging up some hubbub with you or your brothers."

"What're your thoughts then?" Colton crossed his arms over his chest.

Sheriff Tully shrugged. "I see no reason why his claim isn't legitimate."

Lily took a step forward, wanting to take a swing at the sheriff. She closed her hand into a fist. Fury rolled through her body. "This land belonged to my father." She stormed up to the sheriff. "He wanted me to have it."

She leapt forward, about to land her first strike on the sheriff's throat, when she felt an arm wrap around her waist, pulling her back. She fought against the vise-like grip, wanting to smash into the sheriff for taking away what little she had left. "I am no one's property. He can't do this! Colton, tell him he can't do this."

*****

When she looked up at him with those big round eyes full of hope, he wanted to give her the world. The kind of hope which made a man do stupid things. He pulled her back towards the padre. "Just stay put."

He turned back to the sheriff. "Tully, you're too spineless to do what's right. The lady and I were about to come to an understanding in regards to this property."

The sheriff shook his head. "Her father's will was very clear. Everything goes to her husband."

"That's only because Robert forced him to sign it." Lily crossed her arms over her chest.

He glanced back toward her. Though her temper had gotten the better of her, Colton could see the fear in her eyes. Her body shook like a leaf, and damn if that didn't make the need to protect her that much more important.

Sheriff Tully held his hands up in surrender. "Regardless of why he signed it, it still says it goes to her husband."

Colton rested his hand on his gunbelt. "Then I guess we'll be finding that paper and burning it."

"It's under lock and key." The sheriff crossed his arms as if he thought that would deter Colton.

Colton gave a humorless chuckle. "Good thing my brothers have no problems with locks. Isn't that right, Jace?"

"I do believe I could take a crack at it." Jace waved his hand casually.

"And like I said, Luke will have no problem burning up that paper." Colton didn't try to hide the threat in his voice.

Tully stepped up to him, coming almost nose to nose. "Are you threatening me?"

"And if I am?" Colton bumped his chest.

"If I may?" Father Morgan stepped next to them, placing a hand on each of their chests. With a light touch, he pushed them apart.

Colton allowed the priest to push him a step back. Truth be told, if he wanted to, he could've told the good old padre to back off, and he wouldn't mind putting a few holes into the coward of a sheriff. Just looking at his Raven shaking like a leaf twisted something in his gut, and a man can't go against his gut. "Speak quickly, Father."

Father Morgan folded his hands. "The only solution to save this ranch and Lily is if she takes a husband."

"I just got ri—I just lost one husband, and you expect me to take another?" She put her hands on her hips. "No."

Colton looked at Father Morgan. "Who you looking to marry her to on such short notice?" Before he asked the question, he knew the padre had a plan. Men of the cloth always had a plan.

Father Morgan held out his hands in front of him as though he were preaching to a congregation. "The solution seems simple to me. One of you must marry Lily. It would make Daniel's claim to this farm—and Lily—illegitimate."

"The hell you say?" Jace took a step back, his eyes wide. For the first time in his whole damn life he actually looked scared, and Colton had never seen an ounce of fear in his eyes. Being the youngest of seven boys had a way of beating the fear out of you. But the mention of marriage, and Jace damn near looked like he was ready to sprout wings and fly away.

"No." Lily crossed her arms and held up her chin, the way she always did when she meant business.

"Can't say I'm exactly the marrying type, either, Padre," Colton said, though for some reason, the thought of marrying Lily didn't put him off.

"It is the only logical thing to do. You and Lily get to hold a claim over this land, which is what you both want. And Daniel Buckley will have no right to it." Father Morgan shrugged. The man appeared innocent enough, but Colton saw ulterior motives behind his eyes.

"Now, I have to object to this." Sheriff Tully held up his hands. "Ain't no sense in putting Daniel Buckley off."

"If you didn't wear that star over your chest, I'd put a hole in you myself." Jace spat at his feet. "I ain't never seen a man so corrupt."

Tully's face flushed bright red. "Well, I-I-I don't rightly know what you're talking about," he blustered.

"If you ask me, this town needs a new lawman." Colton pulled another hand-rolled from his pocket and lit it. When he looked over at Father Morgan, he saw the barest glint of hope in his eye. Colton had seen the same look before. He could tell the padre wanted a new sheriff, as well.

Tully hiked up his pants. "I do a damn fine job of protecting the folks of this here town."

"So long as it aligns with your pockets." Lily stomped over to Colton and pulled the cigarette out of his mouth. "As much as I love the smell, you're going to pollute your inners."

"You do that again, and I'll put you over my knee." Colton fought to hide the smile she drew from him.

Father Morgan motioned between the two of them. "And there you have it. I do believe you are in need of a good wife, Mr. Sutton."

Lily stomped her foot. "No!"

Father Morgan took Lily's hand, patting it like a child. "My dear, you and I both know, one way or another, a man will be in this house. At least this way, you have a bit of a choice."

"You're forgetting something, Padre. Neither of the men in question here have agreed to this." Colton waved his hand to Jace and himself.

"I'd be more that hap—" the sheriff started.

"No!" Jace, Colton, Lily and Father Morgan all protested in unison.

"It was just a thought." Tully shuffled his feet.

"Lily, do you want to protect your land?" Father Morgan continued to hold her hand.

"Yes." Her chin dropped just a fraction.

"Mr. Sutton, do you share an interest in this land?" He stared at Colton.

In truth, Colton wanted a stake in the area, and Buckley Ranch seemed like the perfect spot. It had all the things he and his brothers would need as they traveled, but it would mean taking on a wife he wasn't ready for. "I believe I do."

"Then there you have it." The padre gave them a both an ear-splitting grin.

"Well, shit. I guess I'm a witness," Jace chuckled.

Chapter 5

Colton had been kind enough to give Lily some space after their quick nuptials. Robert had only died a few weeks ago, and here she was taking on another husband. Though the ceremony had taken place in the mid-morning, Colton insisted on getting the ranch back in working order, so for the rest of the day, he mended fences, tended to the livestock and spoke to Jace all day long. Besides his *I do*, he hadn't said anything to her. She dutifully undressed and slipped into her nightgown, the light cotton hanging loosely from her body, allowing her a small amount of comfort.

At some point during the day, Colton had moved all her things from the small bedroom she used into the largest room on the ranch. She pulled the covers up to her chin and waited. Heavy foot falls echoed down the wood-planked hall toward the door. Her heart leapt up into her throat as the knob on the door turned and Colton stepped through. He took one look at her and quickly closed the door behind him. "You look about as comfortable as a coon in a den full of snakes."

Lily tightened her grip on the blanket. "You didn't have to move my things in here."

"You're my wife now. We stay together." He plopped his hat on the side table and chucked off his boots.

"I could stay in my room." Her words came out much softer than she expected them to.

"That room ain't fit." Colton pulled his shirt over his head, revealing his strong, well-sculpted stomach. His thick body had been honed by years of hard work. . When he lifted his arm to run his hand through his hair, the muscles in his arms stretched and flexed, giving Lily a perfect view of what her husband really looked like. He towered over Robert by far. Whereas Robert had men doing all the work for him, Colton took a more hands-on approach, and it showed in the hard planes of his body.

Lily looked him over from head to toe, taking note of all the scars marring his tanned skin.

He waved a hand in front of her face. "I said, aren't you more comfortable here?"

She shook herself and looked up into his eyes. His lips tilted in a half-smirk like he knew she'd been gawking at him. Lily snuggled farther down into the blankets. "Robert liked his space."

Colton unfastened his belt. The clicking of metal filled the room for a moment. When he hooked his fingers into the waistband of his jeans, he paused, looking down at her. "First thing you need to learn—I'm not Robert. What we got between us starts afresh. You understand?"

She nodded, wanting so much for that to be the case. She was prepared to do her duty to him as a wife, in whatever way that might be. "I understand."

Lily tried to swallow the knot in her throat as he began to inch his pants lower. With a hard yank, he dropped them to the floor and stood before her naked. His manhood stood at attention between them She took a deep breath, nervous he would never fit into her. Her eyes widened as he pulled up the blanket and climbed into the bed. The mattress dipped as he stretched out. Lily's body went stiff as a board. She'd had relations before. Hell, her husband invoked his rights on her even when she didn't want it. But Colton was different. She wanted to please him, to keep him happy. In her experience, husbands who were pleased were less likely to hurt their wives.

Colton reached for her and wrapped his arm around her shoulder. Lily pulled up her nightdress and opened her legs. She pressed her head back against his arm and looked up at the ceiling, waiting for him to climb on top of her. When he didn't move, she looked over at him. "I'm ready."

"Ready for what?" He pulled up the blanket and looked down at her body, his eyes lingering on her breasts then trailing lower over her stomach and between her legs.

"You have rights as a husband."

"That I do, but what goes on in this bed will only happen if you want it to." He pulled her dress over her naked body, covering her up. Lily could see his manhood straining toward her, yet he made no move to jump on her and buck at her like a wild horse.

Her mouth suddenly felt dry, she wet her lips trying to ease her nerves. If she couldn't please him, he'd leave her and the ranch at the mercy of Daniel Buckley. "You can do whatever you want."

He arched his eyebrow at her. "Such as?"

"I can lay very still no matter how hard you want it. I can scream bloody murder without you even having to hurt me."

She closed her eyes, praying she could keep this ranch. Living with Colton wouldn't be so bad, if they could get past this part.

"Shit." He pulled her closer, tucking her head under his and wrapping his arms around her. Lily didn't dare move. He pulled back, looking down at her. "Raven, whatever happens in this bed, it'll be something we both like and want."

She didn't believe him. "Since when does what a woman wants and what a man want go hand in hand?"

"What is it that you want?" He kissed the tip of her nose.

"To be left alone."

"Besides that." He chuckled and ran his fingers through her hair, petting her the way he'd pet a cat. "In the eyes of God, we are married, and as such, we will be husband and wife in all ways. That includes lovin'."

Lily sighed and nodded. When she reached again for the hem of her nightdress, Colton stopped her by resting his hand over hers. "Let's take it slow and see how it goes."

Take it slow? She wanted it over and done with. At her own pace, she dropped the hem of her dress and leaned into Colton. "What now?"

"Now you kiss me, and we see if we can't find some of the fire you showed me last night." He leaned in, brushing his lips against hers. At first, his touches were light teases coaxing Lily to press her lips to his. Still never closing her eyes, she watched every move he made. The blanket surrounded them, blocking his view of her naked body and blocking her view of his body… much to her dislike. She shimmied a little closer,

Colton pressed his lips to hers and allowed his tongue to skim her mouth.

She darted her tongue out, letting them mix together in a dancing heat. Her eyes drifted shut as he wrapped his arms around her and pressed his body up against hers. She felt his stiff length laying against her belly yet he made no move to mount her. She reached out and laid her hand on his chest, testing out how it felt to have a man under her touch. A shudder ran over his body. His fingers flexed and pressed into her skin. A moan escaped her lips. While his hands drifted over the light cotton of her nightdress, she felt him move his grip from around her body to her stomach and higher up toward her breast. He cupped her through the nightdress, brushing his thumb over her nipples, coaxing them into tight, sensitive peaks.

"That's my girl," he praised against her mouth. He looked down at his hands full of her overwhelming curves and smiled. "If I had known you were this... beautiful, I would've been saying those I dos much faster."

A surprised gasp was all she got out before his lips were over her mouth once again. This time, he was not as gentle but firmer and demanding in his way with her. He pressed kisses to her jaw and down toward her ear. He frowned in frustration when he came into contact with the high collar of her night clothes. With feather-light fingers, her unbuttoned each button, pressing kisses to her exposed skin. Lily tilted her head back, wanting his lips all over her. Her body came alive under his touch. Her skin grew warm, her breath heaved in and out as he wrapped himself around her. When he leaned back to give her a moment of space, Lily followed him, turning on her side to face him. "I'll be a good wife to you."

He hummed deep in his throat before pulling her in again. She wrapped one of her legs around his hip, drawing him closer. She wanted to let go of the hardness she held over herself like a shield—she'd led a long, lonely life. Would Colton be the one to finally join her in the dark?

As if he read her mind, he whispered against her lips, "I got you, Raven."

"I'm so tired of fighting alone." A single tear rolled down her cheek. She brushed it away before he could see it.

He traced his finger down the trail she'd wiped away, catching every little thing she did even when she didn't want him to notice. "You don't have to fight alone anymore. I'm not gonna make pretty promises—this is a hard land. But I can promise you, you do not have to fight alone. I'm here."

She nodded, unable to say a word. Instead, she wrapped her arms around him, clinging to him with all the strength she had in her little body. For the first time in years, the hope that she'd be all right sprung in her chest. Maybe she wouldn't have to spend every day of her life fighting and keeping her guard up with Colton by her side. She kissed him with everything she had. Colton reached down and slid her nightdress higher. The material skimmed against her skin like flutters of cotton. His hand slipped up under the edge of her dress. He cupped her slick heat. He parted her around his finger, sliding it back and forth over her. With each gentle touch, she grew wetter. She moaned, throwing her head back into the pillows. When he dipped his finger into her well, she thrust her hips forward, meeting his pumping rhythm.

"That's it, Raven. Show me the heat," he purred in her ear.

Lily wrapped her hands in his hair and tugged on the wild strands. She placed her mouth on his neck and sucked his skin between her lips. He tasted of salt and sun like he'd spent his day in the desert. His tangy flavors slid down her throat as she thrust her hips toward him. When he pulled his fingers free from her, she cried out, hating the loss of the pleasure he brought her. Colton chuckled. "I got what you need."

He palmed his hard length. Lily shifted position to lie flat on her back, wanting to feel him inside of her. Colton pulled her closer to him. "Stay just like this."

"Facing you? But how?"

"Don't you worry your pretty little head about the how, just stay like this and let me take care of you." He kissed her neck as his hand drifted over her thigh and pulled her leg back to where it had been wrapped around his hip.

With an easy thrust forward, he brushed the head of his manhood over her slick folds. She cried out, loving the feel of his skin on hers. Again, he slid himself forward, running it over her wetness but never making a move to enter her. They locked eyes. His desert dust gaze met the emerald sea of her eyes. Lily wrapped her arms around him. As he pressed forward, his hard length caught at her opening. She spread her legs, trying to fit him, but at this angle, it proved to be difficult. Yet Colton held her tightly, his body pressed to hers. He pumped forward, the head of his thick rod penetrating her. Wetness flowed between them, coating her inner thighs. Lily moved her hips, forcing him deeper. She dug her nails into his shoulder as she stretched to fit him.

"That's it," he purred. They began moving in rhythm. Each time he slid farther into her.

"I need more," Lily begged as she held him closer.

Colton look down at her and nodded. He slipped his hand under her and flipped them over. He lay under her with her legs straddling his hips. He smiled up at her. "Take what you need."

She tipped forward, his size too much for her to handle. She pressed her hands into his chest. "I'm not all the way down."

"Just let it happen." He flexed his hips up into her.

She fell forward onto his chest, her hands slipping off to the sides. "I don't think I can do this."

Colton sat up and slid both of them back towards the wall where he leaned his back up against it. "Then we'll do it like this."

He kissed her while he bucked his hips upward. Lily forced her knees wider, spreading her legs to take him as much as she could. When his hands clasped her ass, he pushed her up and down, guiding her over his length, each time getting her a little lower. When his hips finally smacked the inside of her thighs, he moaned deep in his chest. His eyes blazed as he began to pump into her at a furious rate. He wrapped his arms around her, pressing his body to hers. "Damn this nightdress."

He fisted the side of the collar and tore the fabric away from her body, exposing her bouncing breasts to him. Cool air met her flushed skin. Goosebumps covered her body just before Colton latched onto one of her nipples. He ran his tongue over the taught peak and pulled it between his teeth. The sensation did something low in her belly and her inner muscles clenched around his hard, probing length.

He hummed with approval. "Like that?"

"Yes, more." She tilted her head looking up at the ceiling, arching her back to present her breasts to him. He hefted them in his hands. She felt his fingers cupping the underside of her breasts. He took turns lapping at one then the other while she bounced on his delicious manhood. Her hair fell out of its long braid and brushed the top of her hips tickling her, yet she didn't care. With a single-minded focus on Colton and his rod moving in her, she felt her body quicken. Her inner walls clenched around him as she hurtled toward the edge of ecstasy.

"Yes, Lily. Give it to me." He reached down between them and grabbed her, placing pressure on the sensitive little nub he knew would work like a switch to get her going. He held her there, guiding her up and down, driving her forward. Every muscle in her body tightened as she grabbed on to his shoulder for leverage. While her pleasure escalated, she pressed her fingers into his skin. Yet she couldn't seem to let go. Her breath came out in hard pants. She squeezed her eyes shut, threw her head back and screamed his name as she finally hurled into oblivion with only Colton as her anchor. Her inner walls milked his hardness as tiny pulses wracked her body.

Colton lifted her up and flipped her on to her back. Like a train on a track, he railroaded her, banging the bed against the wall. Lily wrapped her legs around his hips and clenched her muscles, holding on as best she could. When he looked down at her, she saw his face hard with emotion, his eyes burning like the desert sun, his lips pressed into a line, and a trail of sweat running down his neck. Like a raindrop, it fell from his collarbone and landed between her bouncing breasts. Somehow, he felt thicker inside her. Her body reacted like it had always been his, quickening once more.

"Again!" Colton demanded as he banged her with long, filling strokes. She felt his hard length from tip to base every time he flexed his hips. Her muscles tightened around him, about to explode once more.

"Oh, God. I feel you, Raven. Come with me. Come!" His rod twitched inside of her, shooting the first pump of his hot seed into her. Lily cried out like he scorched her from the inside out. Her body quickly fell into the arc of ecstasy right behind him. She savored each lashing pulse of his hard length as he pumped into her wet heat. She screamed, convulsing around him as though her well wanted to milk him for all he had.

"Take it all." He spoke between gritted teeth, pumping into her one… two… three more times before he stilled inside of her.

"Holy fu—"

She placed her hand over his mouth. "You shouldn't say such things."

When she dropped her hand, he finished. "Fuck." He rested his weight on his hand, only allowing some of his body to press into hers. "That was something else."

"I gave you the fire, yes?" Lily looked up at him while running her hands over his sweat-soaked back.

"Any hotter, Raven, and we'd be throwin' buckets of water on this bed." He smiled, placing a light kiss on her lips. Lily could already feel the soreness in her body as he pulled out of her and rolled onto his side.

He lay flat on his back with his hands behind his head. As he moved away, a coolness drifted over her body. She sat up, taking her time to swing her legs over the side of the bed. She pulled the blanket to her chest.

"Where you going?"

"I need to clean up." She didn't dare to look over her shoulder at him. She didn't want to see the smug face he was sure to have after she'd given into him so easily.

"The hell you will." The bed dipped as he wrapped his arm around her stomach and dragged her back down. A few tugs later, and he had her draped across his chest, her sensitive naked breasts pressed into his side. He tucked her close under his arm, and with the other hand, he reached down, cupping her sore folds. She didn't dare flinch.

"You're all soft and swollen. Was I too rough on you?" He nudged her with his shoulder indicating for her to look up at him.

When she finally got the courage to draw her eyes upward to look at him, she saw concern etched into his face. His eyebrows drew low over his eyes, causing a small wrinkle between his brows. He pouted his lips. Lily shook her head. "Only a little." She chuckled. "But I liked it."

He bent low, placing a kiss on her lips. "That's my Raven. I like the idea of my seed inside you." He tapped his finger over her sensitive nub.

She squirmed away from his touch, and a dark chuckle rumbled deep in his chest. "Fine, wife. I'll let you rest tonight, but I make no promises about tomorrow."

"Now that sounds like a bargain to me." Lily yawned and pressed her cheek into his chest, drifting off into sleep to the sound of his heart beating under her.

Chapter 6

Colton hunched over the side of the stables, looking for Jace. Damn if he couldn't find the man anywhere. When he peeked into the last stall, he found the youngest Sutton lying up against a bale of hay with his hat pulled low over his eyes. Colton yawned and kicked the side of the stall, jostling Jace right out of his slumber. He leaned over the top of the door. "Damn, boy, you lost?"

"I thought y'all needed some privacy." He rubbed at his eyes and sat up straighter.

Colton nodded and smiled. "Much obliged to you."

"You're one lucky bastard." Jace lumbered to his feet.

"That I am." In truth, Colton didn't know if he'd bitten off the wrong end of the stick by marrying Lily. But after last night and the way she'd woken him up this morning, he'd say he was the luckiest man in the territory. It wasn't every day a man woke up to his wife stroking him while he slept, and then when he cracked his eyes open, she climbed up on his stiff morning rod and rode him to kingdom come. Her hot little sheath slid over his hard length like they were made for each other. Just thinking about it now made him want to go find her again. At this rate, he'd get a babe in her in no time. Jace was mumbling to him, but he couldn't drag his mind away from the thought of what kind of hellion they might have together. A sharp jab to his shoulder brought him back to the present.

"I said... I sent word to our brothers yesterday afternoon."

Colton rubbed at his arm. Normally, he'd leap over the stall door and tear into Jace's hide for that, but today all he could do was smile. "Good. How long you think before they arrive?"

"I suspect a day or two. They'll ride hard to get here."

"Took me two weeks to find you." Colton crossed his arms over his chest. He didn't like only having two men on the land while Daniel Buckley headed toward them to make his claim on Colton's land and his woman.

"How many jails you check between here and home?" Jace opened the stall door and walked out to pat his newly acquired horse.

Colton counted in his head. "'Bout twelve."

"There you have it. They ain't gonna stop. We sent the need for backup. They'll be comin'." The horse bumped Jace's chest. Animals took to him like chubby children took to sweets.

"Who'd you send for?" Colton pulled a smoke from his pocket and held it between his lips. He'd wait until he got outside to light it.

"Jack. Dalton." He sighed, running his hands between the horse's eyes and down to his nose.

"I get the sense you're leaving someone out."

"Luke." Jace looked up at him with blank eyes.

"Shit." Colton kicked at the floor. "He's damn near crazier than the lot of us. And you thought it was a good idea to bring him around Lily?"

"He ain't gonna hurt his kin. He never has and never will. You know Daniel Buckley is one mean son of a bitch. We need him."

"I suppose you're right." Colton crossed his arms.

"I usually am."

Colton shoved him with a playful shoulder bump. "I have to say I didn't realize how few men we have here. We need to start hiring some capable bodies."

"Who can fight." Jace shoved him back.

"And know their boundaries." Colton looked back toward the house where he'd left Lily to dress and get ready for the day.

Jace nodded. "That wife of yours is going to be a handful."

"Don't I know it." Colton chuckled, realizing for the first time he didn't mind taking on the responsibilities of a husband.

An earth-shattering scream broke the comraderie between Colton and Jace. Colton spun on his heels and sprinted toward the house with Jace hot behind him. Only Lily's screams could make Colton's heart stop in his chest. As soon as he stepped out of the barn, he stopped short. At least a dozen guns pointed at his torso, and he stood surrounded by horses and men. At the dead center of the circle, right across from him, sat Lily, a large hand clamped over her mouth and another wound around her waist, holding her still.

Colton spat on the ground, doing his best not to run at the man holding his Lily. "Daniel Buckley."

Daniel stood a head taller than Lily. His deep black eyes matched his hat and jacket. A smile spread across Daniel's lips while a large cigar hung from his mouth. "Colton Sutton, I imagined you to be a much bigger man."

Colton had at least four inches and fifty pounds on Daniel. In a hand-to-hand fight, Colton would kill him. But this wasn't hand-to-hand. Colton was outnumbered and outgunned. "I suppose everyone is bigger to you. Pity."

The smile dropped from Buckley's face. He jerked Lily in his arms. Colton watched as she squeezed her eyes shut and silent tears ran down her cheeks and onto the hand Daniel held over her face. Daniel licked the side of her neck. "Darlin', you taste so sweet. I bet the boys here would love your flavor."

Colton took a step forward. "You keep touching my wife, and I'll cut your tongue out."

"Your wife?" Daniel gave a humorless chuckle. "I think the honey pot just got sweeter. What do you say boys?" The gang surrounding them gave a collective chuckle.

Lily's eyes flashed wide open, then narrowed. Faster than Colton thought possible, she snapped her head back right into Daniel's nose. Blood poured down his face, yet he didn't let her go. He shoved her into the hands of the gunslinger from the other night, Clint. Lily stumbled into his arms, yet continued squirming.

Daniel turned to face Colton. "I have a proposition for you."

Colton never took his eyes from Lily. "Can't say I'm interested in anything you have to say."

"The woman for the land. I'll let you keep her if you sign over my brother's land to me." Buckley took a puff of his cigar. The thick smoke drifted toward Colton. Though it stung his eyes, he stared Buckley down.

Colton took another step forward, but the sound of loaded guns cocking stopped him from not taking another one. He'd be no good to Lily if he got shot. "How about I make you a proposition?"

Buckley arched his eyebrow at him. "Can't wait to hear it."

"How about you take your men and leave before I cut your tongue out for putting it on my wife. Then your hands for touching my wife. If you're very lucky, I'll leave you alive; otherwise it will be a slow, painful death. I'll be sure to send you back to your kinfolk piece by piece."

Buckley tilted his head back, letting a hearty laugh erupt from his lips. "I should kill you right now."

"I don't think today is the day to die, Colton." Jace placed his hand on his arm.

"I'd listen to your brother if I were you." The end of Buckley's cigar flared bright red as he took a drag.

"That's right," Jace encouraged. "Who else can stop Luke from burning them alive? You know he won't listen to me." Jace dropped his hand from Colton's arm and stepped up next to him. "But then again, I always did like a good show."

The men around them shifted uncomfortably. The smiles dropped from their faces. Colton might've been famous for heading up the Sutton Boys, but Luke was famous for his talent with flames. Some believe he'd been born with the devil's gift. The rumors spread like wildfire through the territory. Buckley flicked the ashes from his cigar. "I'll give you two days' time to decide." He looked over at Lily who stood quivering. "I'd be quick if I were you. No telling what a camp full of men might do."

Colton reached for his gun, but Jace placed his hand over Colton's, stopping him from drawing his pistol. "You'll be no good to her dead," he said quietly through gritted teeth.

Buckley strolled toward his horse and swung his leg over the saddle easily. With a snap, he signaled for Clint to hand over Lily. Colton watched as they tossed her over the saddle like a basket of hay. She sat up looking at Colton with sadness in her eyes. He'd let her down. The knowledge would damn near kill him for the rest of his days. He caught her eye. "I will come for you."

Buckley tied a gag around her mouth, the black material a stark contrast to her pale skin. She shook her head as tears poured down her face. Buckley dug his heels into the side of his midnight horse setting the beast forward at an unholy speed. One by one, his gang followed him, leaving a trail of dust in their wake. Colton shook from head to toe as waves of fury lapped at his insides. He shoved Jace to the ground and jumped on top of him. "How the hell did they get in here without us knowing?"

"I don't know!" Jace grabbed Colton's shirt and pulled him closer. They were nose to nose. "We will get her back."

"For the sake of this land, we'd better. Otherwise, I will be embracing the name Satan's Sons." Colton shoved off him and stomped toward the stables.

"Where are you going?" Jace followed behind him.

"After her." Colton marched into Scorpion's pen and began to saddle him up.

"Think about this—that's what they'll expect. You go at them head on, and you'll get yourself killed... and Lily."

Colton gritted his teeth. "Then what do you want me to do? Sit here and wait for them to rape and kill her?"

"No, we scout it out. They must've come in through the rock face at the back of the ranch. There has to be an opening somewhere. Let's find it, keep an eye, and wait for the others to form a plan."

"And then what?" Colton stared Jace down.

When Jace looked back at him, a cold, dead smile broke across his face. "Then we introduce them to their maker... or ours."

Colton's Ambush

Chapter 7

Daniel Buckley sat across from her with the same smug smile his brother used to give her. The fire crackled between them, yet neither of them spoke. Lily crossed her arms, covered in filth, blood and God only knew what else. It had been a full day and a half since she'd been taken from Colton, and he still hadn't come for her.

Buckley leaned back against the log in the cave they occupied. He lit the end of his cigar with a twig from the fire. "Don't think your man is coming for you."

Lily narrowed her eyes at him and crossed her arms. "He'll come."

A deep, belly rolling laugh broke free from Buckley's lips. "If I were him, I wouldn't. That land is dead center of the territory. Perfect for cattle drivin'. Whoever owns that gets a major stake in the market. A small fortune, if you will. I can't see how you're worth that much trouble. I see why my brother married you. You're something to look at, and you come with land. But the trouble just ain't worth it." He paused, staring at her. "They say he died suddenly. His heart just stopped or something. Is that true?"

Lily shrugged and looked down at her hands. "Who can tell why people die these days." She brushed away the dirt on her dress. The blue cotton hung in tatters from her body. She couldn't stand to look at Buckley, not when his words felt like a slap in the face. But sitting here like a timid kitten is not what Colton would want. She looked Buckley dead in the eyes and lifted her chin. "He'll come, and when he does, you'll be joining your brother."

The smirk dropped from his face as he rose to his feet and came around the fire to squat in front of her. He grabbed her face, squeezing it between his fingers, pressing her cheeks into her teeth. The tangy taste of blood sprang in her mouth. She refused to cry out. Instead, she stared at him, showing him exactly how cold and dead her insides could be.

His tilted his lips in a snarl. "It's nearly sundown. I'd rest up if I were you. It's going to be a long night. More of my men have been hankering to meet you." As he leaned in, his hot breath drifted over her face, bathing her in the scent of rotting teeth and cigar smoke. "These ones won't be so gentle as the ones from last night." He shoved her face away, knocking her into the dirt.

She spat the blood from her mouth. "None of your men came near me last night… I survived."

"Survival is no longer my concern. They would've been real gentle-like. But now, it's clear your man isn't coming, and I've no use for you." He looked her body up and down. "Except for one." He hiked up his pants. "Hell, I might be first."

He strode from the cave like he owned it, leaving Lily surrounded by stone walls. If she didn't know better, she'd think Colton might've left her. If she didn't know better.

*****

If a man could be near the brink of insanity, it was Colton. He hadn't eaten in two days, he was on his last hand-rolled

76

smoke, and if he didn't get to his woman soon, death would be upon this territory faster than a twister. Hell hath no fury like a man parted from his wife. "I'm tired of waitin'," he groused.

"The sun will be down in moments." Luke hung in the shadows of the cliff face they occupied. His inky hair was barely visible in the twilight, while his dark duster hung down to his ankles, wrapping him in blackness. He peered over at Colton with cold, ice blue eyes.

Colton remembered Luke's eyes used to hold all the life of the world in them, until he'd lived through hell. He didn't know another man who could handle dynamite the way Luke did. Not an ounce of fear showed in his face. Some say he feared nothing. Others said he welcomed death with open arms. Then there were those who thought him to be death itself. Before meeting Lily, Colton didn't know what to believe, but standing here now with panic eating at him, he knew one thing would save his brother—a good woman.

"You thinking about taking a swing at me?" Luke fiddled with the stick of dynamite in his hand, toying with the wires.

Colton shrugged. "Not particularly."

Luke tossed the dynamite in his hand end over end then caught it. "Good."

Colton took a small step back. "You wanna be doing that? Dynamite ain't stable."

"Nope, it's not." He tossed it up and again and caught it.

"You got a death wish?" Colton took the dynamite from his hand.

Luke stepped up to him, coming chest to chest with him. Colton had always been the larger man, but standing this close to Luke, he realized he younger brother had the advantage in both size and weight. Luke took the stick back from Colton. "You don't want to be messin' with that. I've rigged it just right. You play with it, and it's likely to go off before we want it to."

Thinking about an explosion this close to Lily set his nerves on edge. He turned from Luke and paced back and forth next to the ledge. "You think this'll work?"

"It'll put a right big hole in the back of the cave she's being held in." Luke look across the ravine toward Buckley's camp. "You still gonna want her after what they probably did to her?"

Colton stopped his pacing and leapt at Luke, pinning him to the wall so hard he heard the wind whoosh from his lungs. The stick of explosives dropped to the ground at his feet. He shoved his elbow up against Luke's throat. "I want her no matter how she comes back to me."

Determination to see Lily home safely overcame him. He'd want her no matter how many men had gotten to her. But if he wanted to get her back alive, then he needed to live long enough to get her. Walking into an uphill battle alone against Buckley's crew would've been a surefire way to get himself killed.

Luke held his hands up at his sides. "Brother, I'm with you." He tapped Colton's arm, still on his neck. "I'm with you."

Colton backed off. "Good." He shook himself. "All right, we need to do this." If a madman tried to pretend he had an ounce of sanity, he would be acting like Colton. He let Luke go and took a larger step back. Embarrassment overwhelming him, he stared at his feet. "I need her. I can't explain it."

When he glanced up into Luke's icy eyes, he saw they were filled with determination. Luke nodded his head. "Then we'll get her."

The last rays of sunlight disappeared behind the horizon, blanketing them in the cover of darkness. Luke bent down, picked up the stick, and placed it in his back pocket. "You ready?"

For the first time in two days, Colton felt calm and steady. He nodded while checking his guns. He pulled the large blade from the belt loop at his back. A grin spread across his face. "I'm ready."

"What's the knife for?"

"I promised Buckley I'd cut out his tongue. I keep my promises." Colton puckered his lips, sending out a low, long whistle as a signal to Jace who waited on the other side of the canyon with two of their other brothers, Dalton and Jackson.

Luke's lips pulled up in an wide grin. "Something tells me a lot of people are gonna die tonight."

Colton shrugged. "They don't call us Satan's Sons for nothing."

They climbed the back of the cliff face to the weakest point in the cave holding Lily. They moved silently through the night. Each step he took over the rocky terrain brought him closer to her. Off to his right, he heard a body drop to the ground with little more than a scuffle. Snapping necks had always been one of Jackson's favorite ways of killing. To his left, a spray of wetness hit the ground. Dalton was always quick with a knife.

Luke gave a light chuckle before he whispered, "Reminds me of the old days." He wedged the dynamite in between two large boulders and started to climb back from it. Colton pressed his ear to the cave wall, hoping to hear Lily's voice. What he heard instead made him want to set fire to the world. A blood curdling scream echoed out from the opening. He jumped down off the ledge and ran back toward Luke. "Blow the damn thing!"

Jace yelled from just outside the cavern. "Now is that any way to treat a lady?"

Leave it to him to take a head-on approach. Gunshots rang out into the night as another scream echoed off the cliffs around them. A cold sweat broke out over Colton's skin as Luke lit the fuse of the dynamite.

It sparked to life just as Luke got a crazed look in his eyes. "Hold your ass."

*****

Lily held up her fist as Daniel Buckley came at her. He reached out and snagged her around the waist, dragging her back. Lily went with him, shifting her weight into her heels. They fell back toward the wall. No doubt he expected her to fight, but when she didn't, he tripped over his own feet, sending them quickly toward the hard, rocky wall. She threw her weight into the direction they were going, slamming Buckley's back into the stone surface.

A puff of his foul breath hit her hair as she struggled against him. His grip loosened for a moment, and she took full advantage. Lily planted her feet and sprung up, snapping her head under his chin right into his throat. His hands dropped away from her waist. She scrambled away from him toward the other side of the cave.

He stood up straight with his hand wrapped around his throat, sweat running down the sides of his round face. He chuckled darkly. "Oh, when I finally get you, it's gonna be that much sweeter."

Daniel dove over the fire at her. Lily tried to sidestep him, but he caught a piece of her skirts and brought her down to the ground with him. A scream burned up her throat and through her lips as she kicked out at his face. Her heel connected with the side of his head but not hard enough to dislodge him. He crawled up her body and straddled her waist, pinning her to the ground. With everything she had, she clawed at him, but his size proved to be more than she could handle. He reared up, knocking her hands to the side, and backhanded her across the cheek. She cried out in pain. Black dots swarmed through her eyes as something warm and wet trickled down her cheek.

"Now is that any way to treat a lady?" a voice yelled out from just outside the cave.

She'd recognize Jace's voice anywhere. She opened her mouth to call out to him, but Buckley covered her mouth with his hands, cutting off her words. She squirmed under him, trying to fight free. She bucked and kicked her legs, but any attempt she made to dislodge him failed. Buckley leaned over her. His sweat dripped onto her face. As he spoke, a wad of spit dribbled from his lips into her hair. "My men will kill him."

To punctuate his point, gunshots rang out in the night, echoing around the walls of the cave. She shoved her hands up at Buckley, but he batted them away. Lily spat in his face. "No, they won't. You're as good as dead."

He slapped her again, harder than the first time. A harsh sting bit her across her cheek, down her jaw and into her neck. She fought against the blackness waiting to escort her into unconsciousness. She looked up into his black eyes, and rather than cry, she laughed. With each chuckle, she let go of her fear, because Colton would always come for her.

A loud explosion rang out from the back of the cave. It was like a thunderclap right above her head. Shards of rock flew in all different directions. The walls around them shook as though a twister had landed on them. The ceiling crumpled, shaking the earth beneath their feet. Buckley threw his hands over his face as Lily grabbed him and pulled him over her body to shield herself from the debris. Dust flew at them in a pillowy cloud as the walls shook. From just outside the cave, gunfire burst to life. The sound of bullets ricocheting made Lily want to run for cover even though she was pinned beneath Buckley. Three men rushed into the cave and hid behind the fallen boulders. Their guns drawn, they fired random shots out into the night.

A bulky crater fell from the ceiling towards her head. She ducked under Buckley, letting the crater fall directly on the back of his head. With a wet smacking sound, Buckley slumped listlessly over her. His weight nearly suffocated her as he pressed into her body.

A maniacal laugh followed the explosion. "Hot damn!" A voice she didn't recognize cheered as he came closer. She gasped for breath, waiting for someone familiar before she called out.

"Damn it, Luke. If anything happened to her, I'll kill your crazy ass." Colton ran headlong into the cave. "Raven? Raven?... Lily?"

The thugs turned toward the back of the cave and fired. Quiet surrounded them as Lily's heart stopped in her chest. Had Colton been shot? She struggled to shove Buckley off her. She sat up just enough to be able to see what was left of the shelter. Like an avenging angel, Colton dove from shadows. He flew through the air, tumbling toward cover. Firelight glinted off his gun as he fired at the men cowering behind the boulders. Another man followed behind him, dashing across the entrance.

Colton fired off two rapid shots, both followed by the sound of bodies dropping to the ground. She watched as he stood up straight, aimed his gun squarely at the last man, and shot him right between the eyes.

She stretched her hand up and waved it. "Colton?" She barely heard her own voice.

The footsteps rushing toward them stopped dead. Colton whispered, "Did you hear that?"

"Yeah," the unfamiliar man answered.

"Lily?"

His face popped into her view over Buckley's shoulder. She smiled up at him. "I knew you'd come."

He reached over Buckley's shoulder and brushed his hand down her face. "Always." He looked back over his shoulder. "Luke, come help me get him off her."

As they pulled Buckley's weight from her, he groaned but didn't wake up. Colton pulled her to her feet and crushed her to him. He ran his hands over her. "Did any of them hurt you?"

Lily shook her head. "Nothing I can't live with." He touched his rough hand gently to her cheek. Pain shot from where she'd been slapped. "Well, I might need some healing."

Luke hauled Buckley to his feet. His eyes rolled in his head until he focused on Lily. Buckley's face drew into in a sneer. "You bitch."

She took two steps away from Colton, hauled back her hand and let it fly at Buckley's face with all the strength she had. His head snapped back with the force of the slap. The nerves in her arm shook. "I might as well earn the title."

Luke dragged Daniel toward the entrance where the gunfire had died down. Colton pulled Lily into his arms and pressed her to his chest. "I need you, my Raven. I don't know what I would've done if something happened to you."

"What are you going to do to him?" She hitched her chin toward the door.

"Exactly what I promised to do. Cut out his tongue and give him a slow, painful death."

"Good." She wrapped her arms around Colton, taking a deep breath, letting the smell of him invade her senses. "But first, I have something to tell him."

Lily walked over to Buckley and whispered in his ear. A shocked breath left him. His eyes flared. "You little whore!"

He broke free of Luke's grip and began to run at her. A firm hand yanked her to safety. Lily stumbled behind Colton. He drew his pistol and fired a shot into Buckley's shoulder, stopping him from advancing. Luke tackled from behind, forcing Buckley to the ground. Even with blood pouring from his wound, he fought against Luke. Kicking out his legs and arms, he pulled himself across the rocky ground toward Lily. Colton took a step forward and launched his foot across Buckley's face, knocking him unconscious. Lily ran to Colton's side and wrapped her arms around his waist. When he pulled her face close into his chest, his breath heaved as he hugged her. "Next time you're going to piss off a killer, let me tie him up first."

Chapter 8

Lily stood in the middle of town, her arms crossed over her chest, her lips turned down in a pout. Her hat sat tilted on her head, and her luggage leaned up against her leg. "Colton Sutton, I'm gonna kill you."

The sight of her always did weird things to his body. But right now, his heart broke in two at the thought of not seeing her again. He loved the way she sassed his brothers, and the playfulness in her eyes each time she did. He'd do anything to make sure she stayed that way. "This is the only way to keep you safe."

Her raven hair ran in waves down her back and over her shoulder. She narrowed her emerald eyes at him. The bruises on her face had faded in less than a week, yet the memory of them haunted him two months later. Her burgundy dress fluttered in the midday breeze. He ran his eyes over her tiny body, already missing her curves and the way they felt in his hands. He was going to miss her smile, the smart way she dealt with him, and the tenderness she'd shown him over the past few weeks. She put her hands on his hips. "I can more than take care of myself. You cannot ship me off to my uncle."

Colton grabbed her and held her closely, pressing his lips to her forehead. He inhaled her honeysuckle fragrance. "I'm your husband. It's my job to keep you safe. Living with the Suttons will only bring more trouble to your doorstep."

"You never asked me what I whispered to Buckley before you killed him."

What the hell? He never asked because he wanted to afford her some privacy. "What does that have to do with you leaving?"

She wrapped her hands in the collar of his leather duster and pulled him low enough to whisper in his ear. "Haven't you heard, Mr. Sutton? I killed my husband."

His heart leapt into his chest. "Wait... He didn't die of natural causes?"

She shook her head, her lips parting into a breathtaking smile. "So, you see, I am more than capable of taking care of myself. I just choose to keep *you* around." She kissed him on the cheek and turned away.

"Well, I'll be damned," he mumbled as the stagecoach headed East pulled away without her. Lily walked by, waving at the people leaving the town, her dress fluttering out behind her.

Luke stepped up next to Colton. "Some woman you got there."

"That she is." He nodded.

Lily turned back toward the men and called out, "Oh, Luke, be a dear and grab my bag for me. The damn thing weighs a ton."

Luke chuckled and tipped his hat. "Yes, ma'am."

She even had the craziest of his brothers somewhat in line. Colton chased after her. When he finally caught up to her, he wrapped her up in his arms. "I love you, my Raven."

She pressed her lips to his. "Always."

23417342R00056

Printed in Great Britain
by Amazon